# FIND YOUR SPARKLE

## BARBARA MORAN

Outskirts Press, Inc.
http://www.outskirtspress.com

Paperback ISBN: 978-1-9772-1904-6
Hardback ISBN: 978-1-9772-1905-3

Cover Photo © 2020 SallyAnn Mickel. All rights reserved - used with permission.

Outskirts Press and the "OP" logo are trademarks belonging to Outskirts Press, Inc.

PRINTED IN THE UNITED STATES OF AMERICA

# FIND YOUR SPARKLE

## By Barb Moran
## Illustrated by SallyAnn Mickel

With Love and Gratitude
to Josephine

This book belongs to

_____

It's the Real me, you see.
The part that will never leave, be sad or hurt.
My forever connection to Love.

When I don't feel good
about myself,
I know I've forgotten
about my sparkle self.

The sparkle deep inside is
where I find Love
And it's Love that brings me back
to feeling - to remembering . . . .

How awesome and unique and
beautiful I am.
How unique and amazing we all are.
Living is feeling.
That's where the gift starts.

I feel sad sometimes, rejection sometimes, shame sometimes.

So I quiet my head and fall inside,
gently connecting to
the sparkle within.
I get through these everyday
feelings and learn to grow.

I just have to remember
that when I'm hurt, it's my
sparkle self that gives me
direction to heal.
That gives me hope in me again,
my world again.

I feel new gratitude each time I am able to move through a challenge and allow myself to find a new place of free that is ME.

It's very special to know
that this is one way -
the most important way -
that we are all alike.

Some of us have just
forgotten about our sparkle.

It's always, always there,
waiting for the moment
that we can remember!

Patiently waiting for us
to find our safety,
our strength and
our beauty.

For our family,

For our friends,

For friends we haven't met yet,

For our pets,

For our food,

For our world . . . .

DRAW YOUR SPARKLE

Can you make this
cloud SPARKLE?

Does the sun SPARKLE?

Color this kitty cat
and puppy dog with
SPARKLE.

Can you color a butterfly with SPARKLE?

Color a caterpillar with SPARKLE.

Even bees have SPARKLE.

The search for our inner light, our truth, begins with a small knowing that we have always had this luminous inner heart space.  My hope is that we will plant a seed for our children (young and old!) to just be quietly aware of this reality.

So many people have journeyed to discover their inner truth, so can teach us how to "fall inside".  Meditation practices have  proven to be the ageless path of our spiritual warrior ancestors to finding inner self, inner being, inner sparkle.   Beginning a meditation practice -without expectation of outcome- can be a clear and promising path to finding your sparkle too!

Finding and honoring your inner light can also be as simple as pausing for moments of gratitude. Take a moment to allow your heart to connect to gratitude…. For our families, pets, food, and Earth.  Breathing in gratitude, joy, or the beauty of what is right in front of us literally changes the energy, the alchemy within us. Igniting this light through gentle daily practice will lead us all to…

BE THE CHANGE!    FIND OUR PEACE!    LIVE OUR LOVE!

FIND YOUR SPARKLE
LIVE YOUR LOVE

As we teach and nurture our children, let's give them opportunities to "see" their sparkle. Allow them to hear often and develop the knowing that their essence is good; that their essence is love. If we give them all the opportunities we can to stay in touch with this natural state of being, we will gradually re-awaken this pure connection within ourselves. Feeling a child's radiance is to feel their pure connection to Love. Let it grow!

For the young adults who are hearing these words for the first time, just allow for the possibility that these words are indeed for you!  Give yourself permission to consider that there is a deeper part of you that is your truth.  The world outside can be a confusing and sometimes even a painful place, but if you don't run away from it, your inner world is calm.  There are plenty of ways to run (including addictions!) but they just take you further away from who you really are.  It's your inner light that makes you special and will connect you to what will make you happy.  It will always wait for you to be ready to see it. Call it sparkle, call it your essence, call it whatever you like…. Just know that you have an inner depth of light that is your amazingness!

CPSIA information can be obtained
at www.ICGtesting.com
Printed in the USA
BVHW010527050220
571442BV00002B/22